The Sad Story of HENRY

by
The REV. W. AWDRY

SCHOLASTIC INC.

New York Toronto London Auckland Sydney
Mexico City New Delhi Hong Kong Buenos Aires

Once, an engine attached to a train

Was afraid of a few drops of rain—

Thomas the Tank Engine & Friends

A BRITT ALLCROFT COMPANY PRODUCTION

Based on The Railway Series by The Rev W Awdry
© Gullane (Thomas) LLC 2001

Visit the Thomas & Friends web site at www.thomasthetankengine.com

ISBN 0-439-33838-7

12 11 10 9 8 7 6 5 4 3 2 1   1 2 3 4 5 6/0
Printed in the U.S.A.
First Scholastic printing, December 2001

It went into a tunnel,

And squeaked through its funnel

And never came out again.

The engine's name was Henry. His Driver and Fireman argued with him, but he would not move. "The rain will spoil my lovely green paint and red stripes," he said.

The Guard blew his whistle till he had no more breath, and waved his flags till his arms ached; but Henry still stayed in the tunnel, and blew steam at him.

"I am not going to spoil my lovely green paint and red stripes for you," he said rudely.

The passengers came and argued, too, but Henry would not move.

Sir Topham Hatt, who was on the train, told the Guard to get a rope. "We will pull you out," he said. But Henry only blew steam at him and made him wet.

They hooked the rope on and all pulled—except for Sir Topham Hatt. "My doctor has forbidden me to pull," he said.

They pulled and pulled and pulled, but Henry still stayed in the tunnel.

Then they tried pushing from the other end. Sir Topham Hatt said, "One, two, three—push," but he did not help. "My doctor has forbidden me to push," he said.

They pushed and pushed and pushed, but Henry still stayed in the tunnel.

At last, another train came. The Guard waved his red flag and stopped it. The two engine Drivers, the two Firemen, and the two Guards went and argued with Henry. "Look, it has stopped raining," they said.

"Yes, but it will begin again soon," said Henry. "And what would become of my green paint with red stripes then?"

So they brought the other engine up, and it pushed and puffed, and puffed and pushed as hard as it could. But Henry still stayed in the tunnel.

So they gave up. They told Henry, "We shall leave you there for always and always and always."

They took up the old rails, built a wall in front of him, and cut a new tunnel.

Now, Henry can't get out, and he watches the trains rushing through the new tunnel. He is very sad because no one will ever see his lovely green paint with red stripes again.

But I think he deserved it, don't you?

Now flip the book over to start another Thomas & Friends adventure.

Thomas the Tank Engine & Friends

A BRITT ALLCROFT COMPANY PRODUCTION

Based on The Railway Series by The Rev W Awdry
© Gullane (Thomas) LLC 2001

Visit the Thomas & Friends web site at www.thomasthetankengine.com

ISBN 0-439-33838-7

12 11 10 9 8 7 6 5 4 3 2 1   1 2 3 4 5 6/0
Printed in the U.S.A.
First Scholastic printing, December 2001

EDWARD, GORDON, and HENRY

by
The REV. W. AWDRY

SCHOLASTIC INC.

New York   Toronto   London   Auckland   Sydney
Mexico City   New Delhi   Hong Kong   Buenos Aires

Edward and Gordon often went through the tunnel where Henry was shut up.

Edward would say, "*Peep, peep*—hullo!" and Gordon would say, "*Poop, poop, poop!* Serves you right!"

Poor Henry had no steam to answer, his fire had gone out; soot and dirt from the tunnel roof had spoiled his lovely green paint and red stripes. He was cold and unhappy, and wanted to come out and pull trains, too.

Gordon always pulled the express. He was proud of being the only engine strong enough to do it.

There were many heavy coaches full of important people, like Sir Topham Hatt, who had punished Henry.

Gordon was seeing how fast he could go. "Hurry! Hurry! Hurry!" he panted.

"*Trickety-trock, trickety-trock, trickety-trock,*" said the coaches.

Gordon could see Henry's tunnel in front.

In a minute, he thought, I'll *poop, poop, poop* at Henry, and rush through and out into the open again.

Closer and closer he came—he was almost there, when crack: "*Whee——————eeshshsh,*" he was in a cloud of steam and going slower and slower.

His Driver stopped the train.

"What has happened to me?" asked Gordon, "I feel so weak."

"You've burst your safety valve," said the Driver. "You can't pull the train anymore."

"Oh, dear," said Gordon. "We were going so nicely, too . . . Look at Henry laughing at me." Gordon made a face at Henry, and blew smoke at him.

Everybody got out and came to see Gordon. "Humph!" said Sir Topham Hatt. "I never liked these big engines—always going wrong. Send for another engine at once."

While the Guard went to find one, the Driver and Fireman uncoupled Gordon, and ran him on a siding out of the way.

The only engine left in the shed was Edward. "I'll come and try," he said.

Gordon saw him coming. "That's no use," he said, "Edward can't pull the train."

Edward puffed and pulled, and pulled and puffed, but he couldn't move the heavy coaches.

"I told you so," said Gordon rudely. "Why not let Henry try?"

"Yes," said Sir Topham Hatt. "I will."

"Will you help pull this train, Henry?" he asked.

"Yes," said Henry at once.

So Gordon's Driver and Fireman lit his fire; some Platelayers broke down the wall and put back the rails; and when he had steam up Henry puffed out.

He was dirty, his boiler was black, and he was covered with cobwebs. "Ooh! I'm so stiff! Ooh! I'm so stiff!" he groaned.

"You'd better have a run to ease your joints and find a turntable," said Sir Topham Hatt kindly.

Henry came back feeling better, and they put him in front.

"*Peep, peep,*" said Edward, "I'm ready."

"*Peep, peep, peep,*" said Henry. "So am I."

"Pull hard; pull hard; pull hard," puffed Edward.

"We'll do it; we'll do it; we'll do it," puffed Henry.

"Pull hard we'll do it. Pull hard we'll do it. Pull hard we'll do it," they puffed together.

The heavy coaches jerked and began to move, slowly at first, then faster and faster.

"We've done it together! We've done it together! We've done it together!" said Edward and Henry.

"You've done it, hurray! You've done it, hurray! You've done it, hurray!" sang the coaches.

All the passengers were excited. Sir Topham Hatt leaned out of the window to wave to Edward and Henry; but the train was going so fast that his hat blew off into a field where a goat ate it for a snack.

They never stopped till they came to the big station at the end of the line.

All the passengers all got out and said, "Thank you," and Sir Topham Hatt promised Henry a new coat of paint.

"Would you like blue and red?"

"Yes, please," said Henry, "then I'll be like Edward."

Edward and Henry went home quietly, and on their way they helped Gordon back to the shed.

All three engines are now great friends.

Wasn't Henry pleased when he had his new coat of paint? He is very proud of it, as all good engines are—but he doesn't mind the rain now, because he knows that the best way to keep his paint nice is not to hide in tunnels, but to ask his Driver to rub him down when the day's work is over.

Now flip the book over to start another Thomas & Friends adventure.